D0069887

WELCOME TO
PASSPORT TO READING
A beginning reader's ticket to a brand-new world!

Every book in this program is designed to build read-along and read-alone skills, level by level, through engaging and enriching stories. As the reader turns each page, he or she will become more confident with new vocabulary, sight words, and comprehension.

These PASSPORT TO READING levels will help you choose the perfect book for every reader.

READING TOGETHER
Read short words in simple sentence structures together to begin a reader's journey.

READING OUT LOUD
Encourage developing readers to sound out words in more complex stories with simple vocabulary.

READING INDEPENDENTLY
Newly independent readers gain confidence reading more complex sentences with higher word counts.

READY TO READ MORE
Readers prepare for chapter books with fewer illustrations and longer paragraphs.

This book features sight words from the educator-supported Dolch Sight Words List. This encourages the reader to recognize commonly used vocabulary words, increasing reading speed and fluency.

For more information, please visit passporttoreadingbooks.com.

Enjoy the journey!

Little, Brown and Company

Hachette Book Group
1290 Avenue of the Americas, New York, NY 10104
Visit us at lb-kids.com

Little, Brown and Company is a division of Hachette Book Group, Inc.
The Little, Brown name and logo are trademarks of Hachette Book Group, Inc.

The publisher is not responsible for websites (or their content) that are not owned by the publisher.

First Edition: September 2015

Library of Congress Control Number: 2015944668

ISBN 978-0-316-30116-9

10 9 8 7 6 5 4 3 2 1

CW

Printed in the United States of America

Passport to Reading titles are leveled by independent reviewers applying the standards developed by Irene Fountas and Gay Su Pinnell in *Matching Books to Readers: Using Leveled Books in Guided Reading*, Heinemann, 1999.

MONSTER 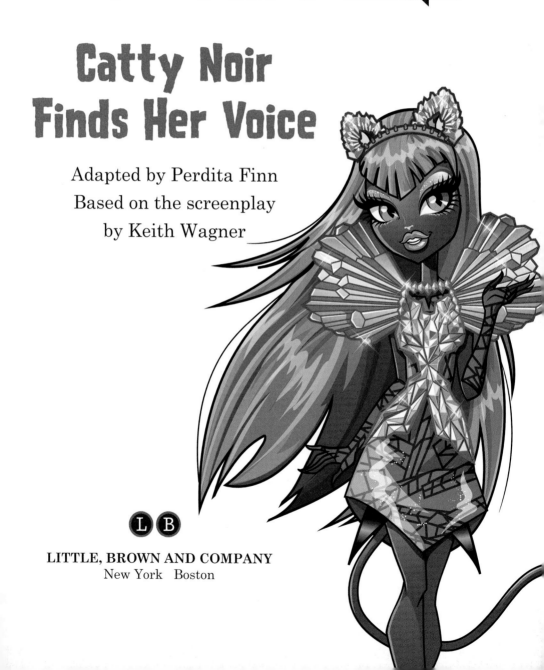 HIGH

Catty Noir
Finds Her Voice

Adapted by Perdita Finn
Based on the screenplay
by Keith Wagner

L B

LITTLE, BROWN AND COMPANY
New York   Boston

Catty Noir is a music star.

She is the princess of pop.

But she doesn't have music in her heart.

"I have to find my own voice."

But Catty is going to Boo York!
Cleo de Nile is taking her ghoulfriends
to the comet gala.

Deuce Gorgon, Cleo's boyfriend,
is going too.

Boo York is exciting!

The ghouls meet Luna Mothews.

"I want to be a star on Bloodway."

Elle Eedee is a robot.

"I am going to DJ the comet gala!"

Madame Ptolemy is
the queen of Boo York.
Her son, Seth, is a prince.
Madame Ptolemy does not like pop music.

Nefera, Cleo's sister, has a plan.
She invites Deuce to brunch,
but she tells him it is a pool party.
Deuce looks silly in his swim gear.

Deuce worries he is not good enough
for Egyptian royalty like Cleo.
"If you love her, you'll leave her,"
says Nefera.

"Get your creeparoni pizza here!"
Luna has her first job as an actress
in Boo York.

But something is wrong with Elle Eedee.
She is hearing music—from outer space!

A street rapper wows the crowd.
"My old name is lame,
so you can call me Pharaoh!"
Catty starts to sing with him.

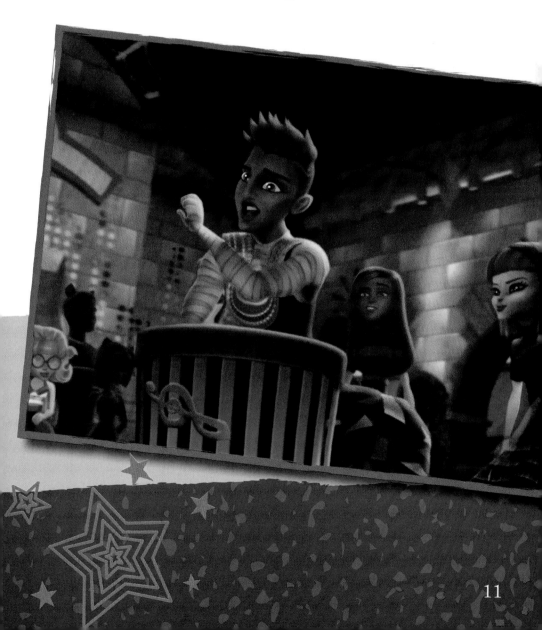

"You are a ghoul, and I am a fool,"
Deuce tells Cleo.
Then he breaks up with her.
It breaks his heart.

Cleo cannot believe that Deuce
would break up with her!

Pharaoh takes Catty
to the Monster of Liberty.
She can hear all the noises of the city.

"I've found my music!" Catty says.
But Pharaoh has to go.
Why can't he stay with Catty?

The ghouls are getting dressed
for the comet gala at the
Museum of Unnatural History!
They are going to look great
on the red carpet.

Someone else is also headed to the party in Boo York.
Maybe the comet isn't a comet.
Maybe it's a...spaceship.

Luna is a waitress at the gala.
Will she ever get to be a star?

Elle Eedee is playing music at the gala.
But she is still hearing something
from outer space!

Madame Ptolemy explains that the comet
visits Earth every thirteen hundred years.
She wants her son to marry one of the
De Nile girls on this special night.
But Seth takes off his mask.
He is really Pharaoh!

"You are the cat's meow,"

Pharaoh sings to Catty.

Now Pharaoh has found his voice too.

Catty joins in!

Nefera's plan is ruined.

She uses a magic crystal to steal

Catty's and Pharaoh's voices.

Then she gives the crystal to

Toralei Stripe to throw in the river!

Pharaoh can't rap anymore.

He is going to put his mask back on.

Will Catty and Pharaoh ever sing again?

At the Hauntson River Bridge,
Toralei is about to throw the crystal
in the river.
But she stops.

"C'mon, rock.
Give me Catty voice!
Toralei wants to sing!"

Deuce pours his heart out
to a haunt dog vendor.
He feels terrible.
He loves Cleo.
Did they really have to break up?

Toralei is onstage,
singing with Catty's voice!
She is stealing the show.

Luna flies to the rescue
and grabs the crystal.
She saves the pop star's voice
from the copycat.
"You are a fright, Tora-liar!"

Catty Noir can sing again,
and Luna is going to be a star
on Bloodway.
She has found her voice too!

Now Deuce and the ghouls have to race
back to the museum.
The comet is coming!

Back at Monster High, Ghoulia Yelps is
also watching the comet.
She sees that it is on a crash course
with Boo York!

Ghoulia plays music to wake up the pilot.
Can she save Boo York?

Catty holds the crystal.
Pharaoh touches his heart
and takes Catty in his arms.
Catty and Pharaoh find their voices,
and they find each other.

"I don't want to lose you."

Deuce finds the courage to tell Cleo what is in his heart.

Cleo snaps a photo.

They are a couple again!

The music wakes up the pilot
of the spaceship.
She is a comet alien.
Her name is Astranova.
She finds what she is looking for
in Boo York too.

All the ghouls at the gala celebrate.
Everyone has a song to sing!

"We are shooting stars, light it up,

be who you are!

We are here to light up the night!

We are shooting stars!

Be who you are!"